# HOOP DANCE HEROES!

## By Karissa Valencia
## Illustrated by Madelyn Goodnight

 A GOLDEN BOOK • NEW YORK

rhcbooks.com

ISBN 978-0-593-64720-2 (trade) — ISBN 978-0-593-64721-9 (ebook)

Printed in the United States of America

10 9 8 7 6 5 4 3 2 1

The Skycedar family is setting up the stage for a special event. Tonight they're hosting a hoop dance show at Xus National Park!

Hoop-dancing is done by many Native American people. The dancers use hoops to tell stories of plants or animals. DeeDee is a great hoop dancer! She smoothly moves the hoops around her body. "This is the eagle move!" she says as she flaps her arms like a bird.

"Wow!" cheers Kodi.
"Amazing!" says Eddy.
"I wanna be a pro hoop dancer!"
exclaims Summer.

"Maybe someday you will," DeeDee says.
"First, let's practice the basics."

"But I don't wanna do the basics," Summer
says with a frown. "I wanna learn the eagle move."
Summer grabs the hoops and tries to twirl them
on her arms. They fall off.

"Once you learn the basics, you'll get to the
eagle move in no time," says DeeDee. "Keep
practicing!" She smiles as she leaves the stage.

Coyote and Lizard join the fun. They love hoop-dancing! "We learned to dance from the spirits," says Coyote.

That gives Summer an idea. "I don't need to learn the basics. I can learn the eagle move from Eagle instead!"

Kodi and Eddy want to learn hoop-dancing from the spirits, too. "Let's go to Spirit Park!" says Summer.

Kodi transforms into Kodi Cub.
Summer transforms into Summer Hawk.
Eddy transforms into Eddy Turtle.
They're Spirit Ranger ready!

In Spirit Park, the rangers meet their new hoop-dancing teachers: Snake, Flower, and Eagle.

"Who's ready to get *sssstarted*?" hisses Snake.

Flower waves at them. "Hoop-dancing is all in the roots!" he says.

"I want to learn the eagle move," says Summer. Eagle spreads her wings. "After you've mastered the other moves, you'll be ready for my move," she says as she flies away.

Snake and Flower teach the rangers their moves.
The hoops form shapes that look like them!

Kodi and Eddy practice and practice and practice. They get better with every try!

But Summer doesn't want to practice the basics. She'd rather learn the eagle move.

After practicing for a while, Snake and Flower say Kodi and Eddy are ready for Eagle's move.

"Finally!" squawks Summer.

Eagle returns and shows them how to spread their arms so the hoops look like wings.

"That looks really hard," Eddy says nervously.

Eagle smiles. "Use what you've learned from Snake and Flower. You can do this," she says.

After a few tries, Kodi and Eddy complete the eagle move! Their practicing worked!

Summer gives it a try, but her hoops tumble to the ground. She didn't practice the basics, so the eagle move is too hard. She hangs her head, disappointed. "I'll never be ready for the show tonight. . . . I quit."

Before Kodi and Eddy can stop her, Summer flies away.

In Xus Park, DeeDee finds Summer in the tree house. "What's wrong, Summer?" she asks.

Summer sighs. "You can do the show without me," she says. "I'll never be an amazing hoop dancer like you."

"Well, did you practice?" asks DeeDee.

"No," admits Summer.

DeeDee smiles. "You have to break everything down into small steps. Then try again and again. That's what practice is," she says.

"I guess I did rush to the eagle move without breaking it down," admits Summer. She gives DeeDee a big hug. "Thanks, DeeDee. I gotta practice. See you at the show!"

Back in Spirit Park, Summer apologizes to
Snake and Flower for skipping over their moves.
"I'm ready to learn. Will you teach me?" she asks.
Snake and Flower smile. "Of course!" they say.

Summer takes the time to practice each move over and over. She gets better every time!

Eagle watches proudly. "Great job, Summer!
Now you're ready for my eagle move."

Summer combines everything she learned
from Snake and Flower . . . and completes
the eagle move! Everyone cheers for her.
"I'm a hoop dancer!" she squawks.

Summer gives her siblings a big hug. "Thanks for helping me practice," she says to her teachers. "I'm ready for the show!"

Back in Xus Park, it's showtime! DeeDee faces the crowd.

"Haku, everyone," she says. "Our hoop dancers have practiced hard for the show tonight. Please welcome Kodi, Summer, and Eddy to the stage!"

The junior rangers show off all their new moves, and the crowd applauds. Thanks to their hard work, they were able to share the beautiful hoop dance stories with the park visitors.
Great work, Spirit Rangers!